For the Auntorage

Copyright © 2018 by Daisy Hirst

First U.S. edition 2018

Library of Congress Catalog Card Number 2018960065
ISBN 978-1-5362-0334-9

19 20 21 22 23 APS 10 9 8 7 6 5 4 3 2

Printed in Humen, Guangdong, China

This book was typeset in WB Natalie Alphonse.
The illustrations were screen-printed.

Candlewick Press
99 Dover Street
Somerville, Massachusetts 02144

visit us at www.candlewick.com

I DO NOT LIKE BOOKS ANYMORE!

Daisy Hirst

CANDLEWICK PRESS

NATALIE and ALPHONSE
really liked books
and stories.

Picture books with Dad,

scary books Mom read when Alphonse was sleeping,

Granny's stories about Melvin Plant Pot and the Terrible Shrew,

and stories
they remembered

or made up.

Natalie said,
"When I can read,
I'll have all the stories in
the world, whenever I want them."

"And you can read them to me!" said Alphonse.

Then Natalie got her first reading book.

"There's a cat in it!"
said Natalie. "I will
read it all by myself."

But when she opened
the book . . .

the letters and words looked
like prickles or birds' feet.

Miss Bimble said, "It just takes practice." She helped Natalie sound out the words. The book was about a cat. The cat could sit.

Natalie tried to read the book to Mom.

"I can't," said Natalie. "And nothing even happens to the cat! I like when you and Dad read to me."

"You will be able to," said Mom.

Dad said, "And the books will get better."

Natalie practiced her reading book all week. Again and again and again, until she knew all the words.

"Now can you read about trains, please, and bears?" said Alphonse.

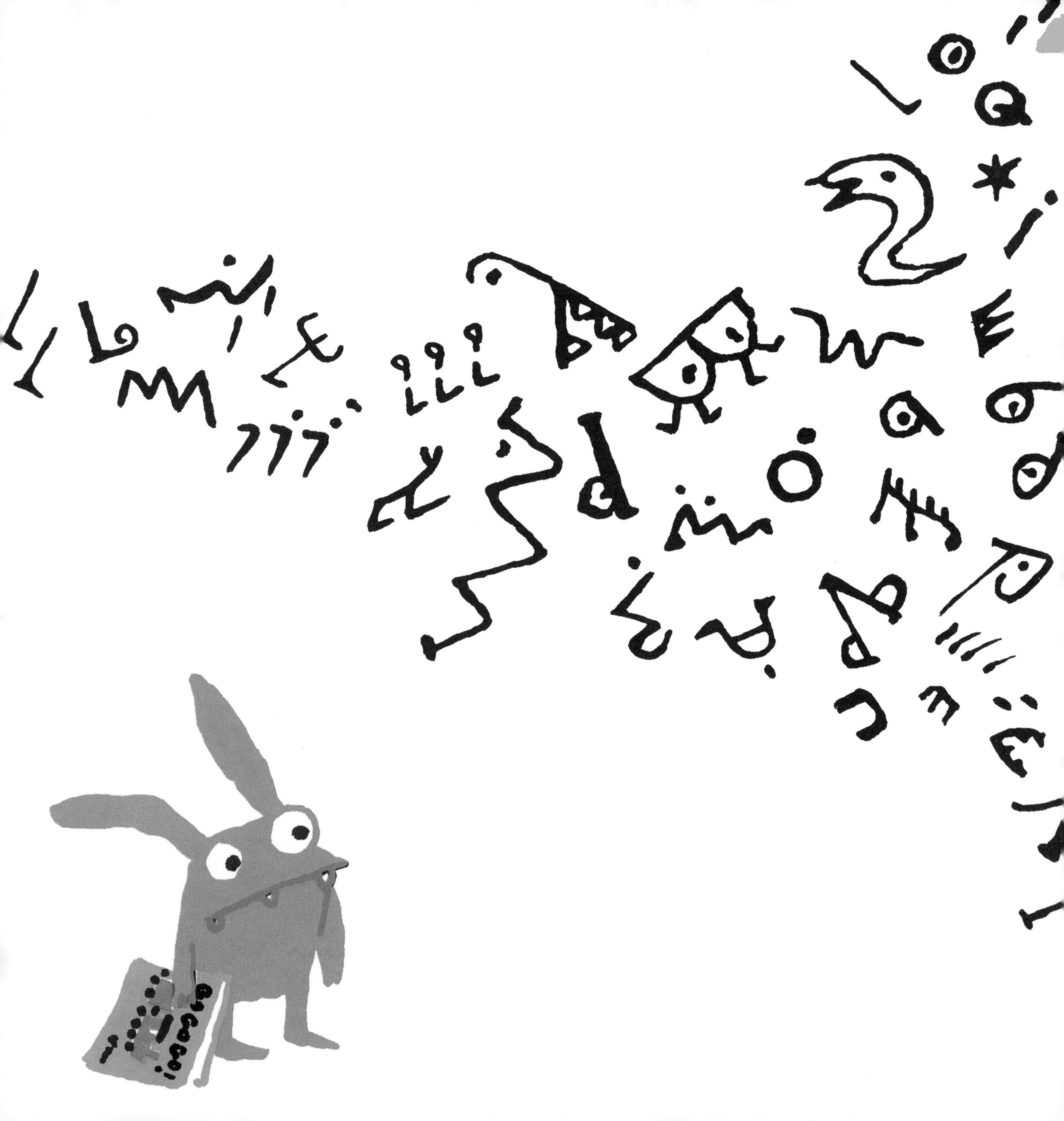

But the letters and words in Alphonse's book looked like scuttling insects, with too many legs and eyes.

Natalie said, **"NO."**

"I DO NOT
LIKE BOOKS
ANYMORE!"

"I can't learn to read anymore," said Natalie. "Sinéad is sick and I have to look after her."

"Poor Sinéad," said Mom. "But you can still learn to read."

"I don't need to," said Natalie. "I can make up my own stories and tell them to Alphonse."

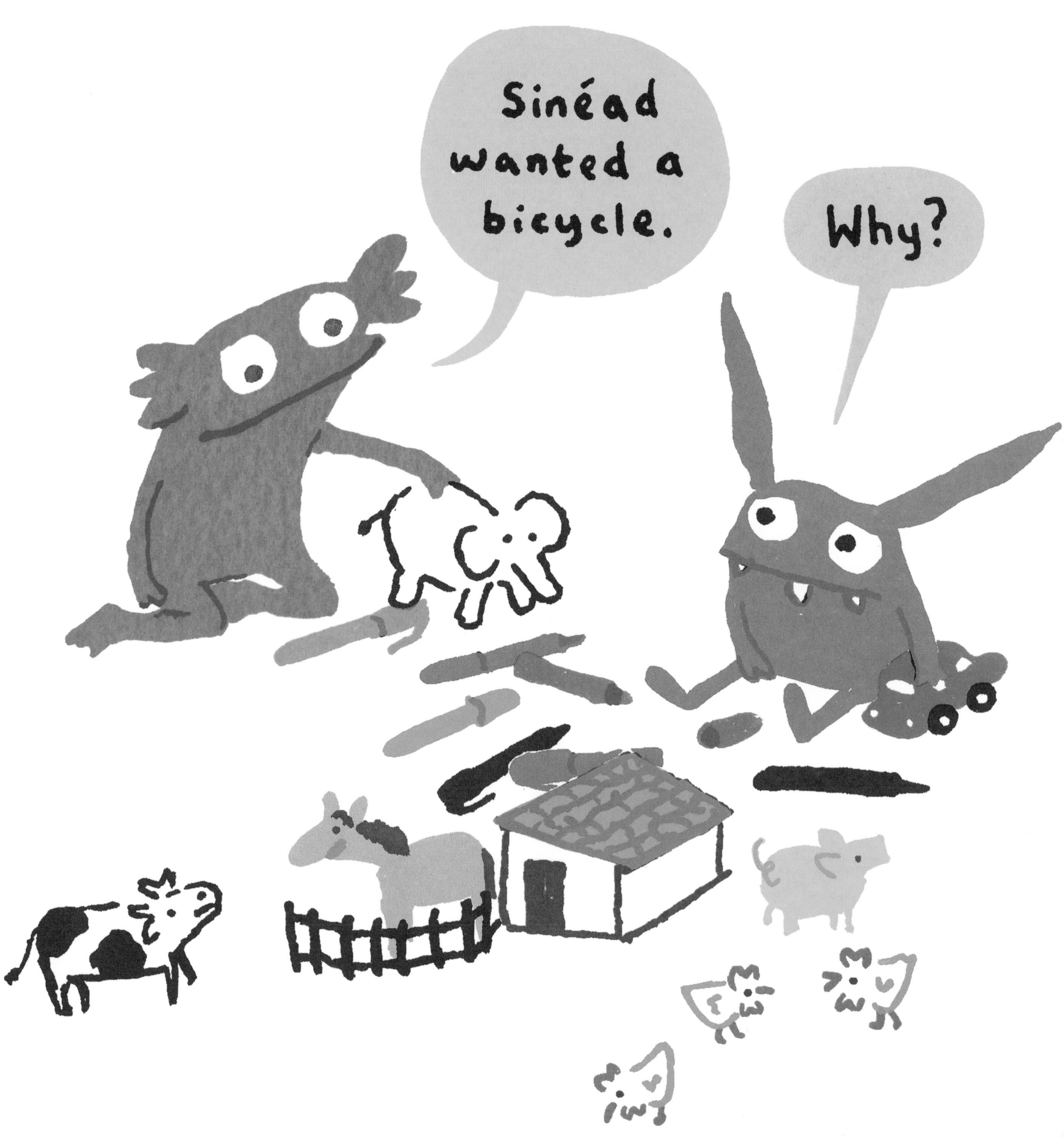
Sinéad wanted a bicycle.
Why?

To go to the farm to see chickens. But she didn't have any money so she had to get a job.

What job?

Cleaning up pens.

Then a caterpillar came in a truck!

OK. A caterpillar came in a truck and ran over the pens.

And it was a MESS and a DISASTER!

Sinéad was so angry, she said, "Eric! You ruined my job! Now how can I buy a bicycle and go to the farm?"

Is Eric the caterpillar's name?

Yes. Eric said, "I know! You can ride in my truck to see the chickens!" And they drove away honking the horn.

"It's a good story," said Alphonse.
"It should be in a book."

"Why?" said Natalie.

"So we could tell it again.
And with pictures."

"Let's draw the pictures
anyway," Natalie said.

Then Natalie told Dad what the words should say, and they stapled it into a book.

"Now can you tell it to me again?" said Alphonse.

And Natalie
found that,
mostly,
she could
read the
book they'd
written

(with Alphonse helping).

BAD CAT
ALPHONSE
Natalie in Space
Whale goes shopp
A Caterpillar Cam in a Truck
BEARS AND JELLY
Natalie and Alphonse's Emergency
Eric Goes to Sea